TICKLISH TIMMY
by TONY GARTH

Timmy was a very ticklish boy. Even the tiniest, weeniest tickle sent him into a fit of giggles.

Timmy's Mum had terrible trouble getting him dressed or giving him a bath. It tickled so much he couldn't stop wriggling or giggling.

Even the thought of being tickled made Timmy laugh.

It sometimes got him into trouble.

Once Timmy and his family went to the theatre to see a show. It was a musical. The curtain went up and the leading lady began to sing her opening song.

Just then, a long feather dangling from a lady's hat tickled Timmy on the ear and Timmy began to giggle. He giggled and giggled, until he couldn't hold his giggles in a moment longer. Suddenly he burst out laughing. The sound echoed around the theatre and made Timmy laugh even more.

The leading lady was not amused. And neither was anyone else.

"Can't you be quiet?" asked a man sitting behind him.

"You're spoiling the show," another man said.

"I think we'd better go home," said Timmy's Dad.

Even the doctor had given up trying to examine Timmy. He had to guess what was wrong from a distance. Luckily, Timmy was hardly ever ill.

Timmy's Dad was a rocket scientist. He was very, very clever indeed. He usually built rockets that went to the Moon. But now he built a tickle-proof suit for Timmy. He used all the latest materials. Unfortunately,...

...it tickled!

On Timmy's birthday, his Mum and Dad threw a big party to celebrate. There were jellies and cakes, and lots of presents. And all Timmy's friends were there.

Korky the clown made a special appearance. Timmy was very excited. He'd never seen a real-life clown before. But Korky the clown just wasn't funny. His magic tricks all went wrong. And nobody laughed at his jokes.

Timmy sighed and took a sip of his lemonade. Some bubbles of fizz tickled the end of his nose.

Timmy began to giggle. Quietly at first, then louder and louder. Then he began to chuckle.

Soon the chuckle turned into a gigantic, roaring laugh. Timmy laughed until his shoulders shook and his sides ached. He laughed and laughed and couldn't stop.

Timmy's laughter was catching. Soon the other children began to giggle and, in no time at all, the whole room was filled with the sound of laughter.

Korky the clown couldn't believe his ears. Spurred on by all that laughter, he gave the best performance of his life. All his tricks worked perfectly. And his jokes were funny, for the very first time.

The children laughed so much that tears ran down their faces.

All too soon, the show was over and it was time for Timmy's friends to go home.

"Thank you. We've had a lovely time," they said to Timmy as they left.

"And thank you from me," said Korky. "I've never enjoyed myself so much. That's the first time anyone's laughed at my jokes."

And he offered Timmy a job as his official assistant.

Wherever they went, Korky's show was a great success. There was plenty of laughter with Timmy around. Timmy could giggle as much as he liked and nobody minded a bit.

And, after the show, he was also allowed as much cake and ice cream as he could eat.

Look out for the next twelve Little Monsters!

FRIENDLY FRANCO

CLUMSY CLARISSA

BOISTEROUS BILLY

SICKLY SIMON

SERIOUS SADIE

GROW GAE

PERFECT PRUDENCE

RUDE ROGER

DANGEROUS DAVE

CURIOUS CALVIN

DIRTY DERMOT

TAN TAB

Printed in Scotland by Waddies Print Group. Tel: 01506 419393.